The Wildlife A·B·C

SIMON AND SCHUSTER BOOKS FOR YOUNG READERS
Simon & Schuster Building, Rockefeller Center
1230 Avenue of the Americas, New York, New York 10020

Text and illustrations copyright © 1988 by Jan Thornhill
All rights reserved including the right of reproduction
in whole or in part in any form.

Originally published in Canada by Greey de Pencier Books
First U.S. edition 1990

SIMON AND SCHUSTER BOOKS FOR YOUNG READERS
is a trademark of Simon & Schuster Inc.

Manufactured in Singapore

10 9 8 7 6 5 4 3 2 1

LIBRARY OF CONGRESS CATALOGING-IN-PUBLICATION DATA
Thornhill, Jan.   The wildlife A-B-C: a nature alphabet / by Jan Thornhill.   p.   cm.
Summary: Introduces the letters of the alphabet through illustrations of a variety of North
American animals and brief rhyming text. Descriptive notes about each animal are included at
the end.   1. Zoology—North America—Pictorial works—Juvenile literature.   2. Animals—
Pictorial works—Juvenile literature.   3. Alphabet—Juvenile literature. [1. Animals. 2. Zoology
—North America. 3. Alphabet.]   I. Title.
QL151.T46   1988   89-19711
591.97—dc20   CIP
[E]   AC
ISBN 0-671-67925-2

The Wildlife A·B·C

A Nature Alphabet Book

by Jan Thornhill

Simon and Schuster Books for Young Readers

Published by Simon & Schuster Inc., New York

Aa

A is for Auk
who lives by the sea,

Bb

B is for Beaver
Felling a tree.

Cc

C is for Caterpillar
Who eats a lot,

Dd

D is for Dragonfly
Flitting by when it's hot.

Ee

E is for Eagle
Seeking salmon to eat,

Ff

F is for Frog
With webbed hind feet.

Gg

G is for Goose
Paddling under a bridge,

Hh

H is for Housefly
Inspecting your fridge.

Ii

I is for Inchworm
Sneaking along the ground,

Jj

J is for Jumping Mouse
Hopping around.

Kk

K is for Killer Whale
In the deep blue sea,

Ll

L is for Loon
Who swims excellently.

Mm

M is for Moose
Munching plants in a park,

Nn

N is for Nighthawk
Catching bugs in the dark.

Oo

O is for Otter
Look at him go!

Pp

P is for Polar Bear

Walking on snow.

Qq

Q is for Queen Bee
Laying eggs to hatch,

Rr

R is for Raccoon
See her lifting the latch?

Ss

S is for Salmon
Swimming up a creek,

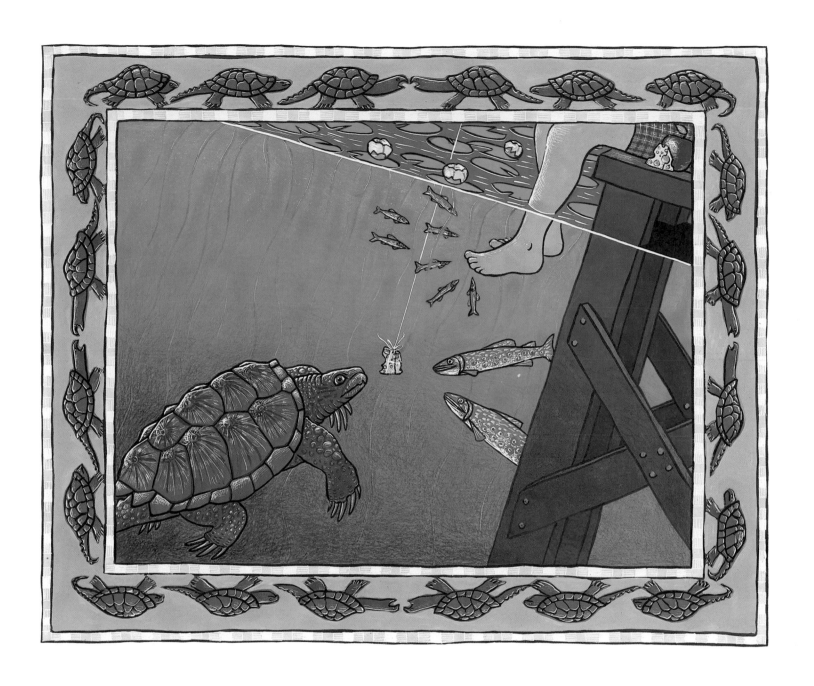

Tt

T is for Turtle
Her mouth is a beak.

Uu

U is for Underground
Who lives there?

Vv

V is for Vole
Who had better beware!

Ww

W is for Whooping Crane
Wading near shore,

Xx

X is for X-ray
Of a big dinosaur.

Yy

Y is for Yellowjacket
Who might live near you,

Zz

And Z is for Zoo!
Can you tell who's who?

Nature Notes

Aa

Great Auk *with a colony of Gannets*

Although there are several smaller species of auk still found in the North Atlantic, the Great Auk is now extinct because of over-hunting. These large, flightless birds were easy prey out of the water and their eggs were collected for food. The last known pair was killed in 1844. Beside them was found a single broken egg.

Bb

Beaver *with a Woolly caterpillar, swimming Beaver, Great Blue Heron*

The Beaver, which is the second largest rodent in the world, has chisel-like, self-sharpening teeth that it uses to cut down trees, remove branches, and strip off bark. After they eat the bark, beavers build dams and lodges with the stripped trees. A beaver's flat tail acts as a rudder in water, helps the beaver balance upright while felling trees, and is slapped loudly on the water's surface to warn the family when danger threatens.

Cc

Black Swallowtail Caterpillar *with eggs, chrysalis and adult butterfly*

Caterpillars hatch from eggs laid by butterflies and moths. In this, the second of its four life stages, the insect devours large quantities of plant matter. Because the Black Swallowtail caterpillar prefers plants such as cultivated carrots, parsley, celery and dill, it is often found in backyard gardens. Over several weeks of intense feeding, the caterpillar increases greatly in size before pupating into a chrysalis. There the adult develops, emerging finally as a butterfly.

Dd

Dragonfly *with Mergansers and pickerelweed*

Dragonflies, with their large eyes, moveable heads and ability to fly both forward and backward, catch huge numbers of mosquitoes and other flying insects. Their eggs, usually deposited on the water, hatch into naiads, the dragonfly's larvae. After several years of eating other aquatic creatures, the naiad crawls out of the water and the fully-formed adult emerges from a slit in its back.

Ee

Bald Eagle *with eaglets in nest, Humpback Whales breaching, Sea Lions basking*

Bald Eagles, who mate for life, build huge nests (some weigh two tons) in tall trees. The young eaglets are fed fish, which their parents catch with their long, curved claws. After the eaglets grow their first dark brown feathers, they learn to fly by exercising on the wide platform of their nest. The Bald Eagle has become an endangered species in many areas because much of the forest in which they find nesting trees has been cut down for lumber or development.

Ff

Leopard Frog *with Ladybug, Ant, White Admiral Butterfly*

The Leopard Frog begins its life underwater as one of a mass of jelly-protected eggs. It hatches into a tiny tadpole which breathes through gills like a fish. Eventually, legs and lungs develop and, soon after, the tail is re-absorbed into the body to feed the final metamorphosis of tadpole into frog who can leave the water to breathe on land. The Leopard Frog has long, muscular hind legs for hopping and webbed feet for swimming, so that it can escape predators both on land and in the water.

Gg

Canada Goose *with Black Squirrel, Cardinal*

The unmistakable honks of Canada Geese ringing across the sky as they migrate in V formation inspired the Cree Indians to call them "hounds of heaven". In the spring, while the goose sits on her two to nine eggs, her mate for life, the gander, stays close by on guard. When the hatchlings appear, both parents stand near so the goslings will recognize them in the future and, because the young identify with the first creature they see, will realize that they too are geese. In the following weeks, the downy yellow brood, which can leave the nest right away, will learn by imitating their parents.

Hh

Housefly *in its most common habitat*

Because they can easily adapt to different environments, houseflies are found all over the world. Their large, curved, compound eyes are made up of about 4,000 hexagonal lenses, each of which points in a slightly different direction so that each sees only part of an object. This confusion of images is joined together in the fly's brain, making one coherent picture. The housefly's two single wings, which distinguish it from other flying insects, can beat 200 times a second.

Ii

Inchworm *with Monarch Butterfly, Nuthatch, and asters, milkweed, burdock, plantain, goldenrod, dock*

Inchworms, also known as measuring worms or loopers, are the larvae of one of the largest families of moths. Their unique way of moving developed because of their lack of legs in the middle segments of their bodies. Some inchworms resemble twigs when they grip a branch with their hind legs and let their long bodies project out on an angle. If they keep perfectly still, this trick of mimicry can fool predators.

Jj

Woodland Jumping Mouse *with a Moth, Owl*

The Woodland Jumping Mouse has large hind legs and a tail longer than its body to help it balance when leaping about, sometimes 2m (6′) in a single bound. Good swimmers, Woodland Jumping mice live in burrows close to water, eating seeds, berries and insects. They are most active at night, when they must be wary of owls, one of their major predators.

Kk

Killer Whale *with Herring Gulls*

The highly intelligent Killer Whales, some 8m (25′) long, and weighing six tons, travel in pods of three to 50 animals, although about ten is the most common number. These tight-knit family groups can be told apart by the different noises, calls and piercing sounds they make. They eat mostly cod, herring and salmon, but will also hunt sea birds or seals, and on occasion will even attack other whales.

Ll

Loon *with Lake Trout, Yellow Perch*

On clear northern lakes in the summer, the cackling, yodeling and haunting wails of the loon are a familiar sound. Such specialized diving birds that they cannot walk properly on land, loons are very fast and agile underwater, capable of traveling several hundred metres before surfacing for air. Their diet consists mainly of fish, but they also eat leeches, crayfish and frogs. Although loon chicks can dive within a day of hatching, they are fed by their parents for several months. If danger threatens, the chicks are carried away on a parent's back or tucked under a wing.

Mm

Moose *with diving Kingfisher, Flicker on tree trunk, Dragonfly*

In the summer, moose are often seen feeding on underwater and floating plants such as pond lilies. Excellent swimmers and divers, it is not unusual for them to stay submerged for a full minute or to swim across a wide lake. The distinctive antlers of the males, which can span 2m (6'), grow anew each year. After shedding the velvety skin which feeds their growth, they fall off in the autumn, and a new set begins growing in by spring.

Nn

Nighthawk *with Bats, Luna Moth*

Nighthawks, which are not true hawks, are most often seen at twilight and after dark, flitting high above city buildings or over open fields. Flying with their huge mouths agape, they can capture large numbers of mosquitoes in a single snap or snatch up a large moth. Nighthawks have adapted easily to city life, laying their eggs on gravel-covered roofs, perfect camouflage for the mottled coloring of the shells.

Oo

River Otter *with Rose-Breasted Grosbeaks, White-Tailed Deer, two Otters playing in river*

River Otters, long and streamlined with webbed feet and waterproof fur, are wonderful swimmers, spending much of their time in water frolicking and catching fish. They are playful all their lives, and enjoy slipping down mud slides in summer and sliding down snowbanks in winter. Two cubs are born each spring in a riverbank tunnel. The cubs stay a long time with their mother, learning from her the skills they will need to survive on their own.

Pp

Polar Bear *with cubs, Arctic Hare, Snowy Owl*

In fall, the female Polar Bear digs a snug den in a snowdrift. There she gives birth to two cubs weighing barely ½ kg (1 lb.) each. In the early spring, when the cubs have grown to about 12 kg (25 lbs.), the mother brings them outside. They stay with her for two years, traveling great distances across the arctic landscape, learning to hunt seals for themselves.

Qq

Queen Honeybee *with attendant workers*

Although there may be several thousand worker bees and several hundred male drones in a hive, there is only one queen. Attended by workers, the queen can lay 1,000 eggs a day. When the eggs hatch, some of the larvae are chosen to become queens and are fed a special diet of "royal jelly" instead of the worker mixture of pollen and honey. In late spring, the reigning queen leaves the hive with a swarm of workers to found a new colony. Soon after her departure, the first young queen to emerge takes the old queen's place.

Rr

Raccoon *with young*

The raccoon roams at night and is an omnivore, meaning it will eat almost anything. In the wild its favorite foods are crayfish, bird and turtle eggs, freshwater clams, nuts and seeds. The young, born in the spring, spend as long as a year with their mother. The raccoon has adapted easily to urban life, showing great dexterity and ingenuity in opening doors, latches and garbage can lids to get at food inside.

Ss

Sockeye Salmon *two males, one female*

Salmon lay and fertilize their eggs in the same freshwater spawning grounds where they themselves originated. After the eggs hatch, the young salmon spend one to three years in fresh water before swimming to the sea, where they remain for several more years. When the time comes for them to make their return journey to the breeding streams, Sockeye Salmon change color from silvery blue-green to red, and their heads turn green. The male grows a hump on its back and its jaws enlarge. Both males and females swim vast distances – battling currents, jumping up waterfalls and evading natural enemies such as grizzly bears – to reach the spawning grounds where the cycle begins anew.

Tt

Snapping Turtle *with Minnows, Brook Trout*

The Snapping Turtle, which lives in ponds, marshes, rivers and lakes, has a long, flexible neck and sharp, powerful jaws that help it catch food. It eats fish, frogs, small mammals, waterfowl and plants and is also a good scavenger. Although the Snapping Turtle can be aggressive on land where it is vulnerable to attack, in its water habitat it is usually shy and unthreatening to humans.

Uu

Underground *with a Meadowlark, Earthworm, Shrew chasing Beetle, Ants, Larva, Millipede, Cottontail Rabbits, Field Mice*

Many creatures spend at least part of their lives underground. Earthworms tunnel constantly, passing large quantities of earth through their bodies, digesting only the dead plant material they need. The shrew digs for insects, its favorite food. Ant colonies build networks of tunnels joined to storerooms and nurseries. Other insects spend either their larval stage (some eating tender root tips), or pupal stage underground. Some mammals, such as mice, dig burrows where they store food, nest and sleep, protected from above-ground enemies. The cottontail, instead of digging for itself, takes over another animal's abandoned burrow to nest in.

Vv

Meadow Vole *with a Fox, Hare, Red-Tailed Hawk*

Meadow Voles live in fields, eating seeds and vegetation. They are fast breeders, producing large litters which mature quickly. Unchecked, a single pair of voles can have 200 descendants in a year. Some years are called "vole years" when their population skyrockets, attracting many predators such as hawks, owls and foxes. To make their movement from place to place almost invisible from above, voles make covered runways – in summer they trample grass and eat away only the lower stems of plants along their routes, and in winter they dig tunnels through the snow.

Ww

Whooping Crane *with Monarch Butterfly, Dragonfly, Turtle*

Whooping Cranes have a remarkable courtship dance which few people have opportunity to witness, because this bird is so rare. In the early 20th century, hunting and the destruction of its habitat decimated the species, and by the 1960s there were less than twenty left world-wide. Fortunately, with help, their numbers are currently climbing, and more whoopers complete the southerly migration to their wintering grounds each year. This majestic bird has a very long, coiled trachea which enables it to make a loud trumpet call that carries across vast distances.

Xx

X-ray of Triceratops *with a Stegosaurus, Tyrannosaurus, Hadrosaurs hatching, Brontosaurs grazing*

During the Mesozoic era, 225 to 65 million years ago, dinosaurs were the dominant animal on Earth. These reptiles came in all different sizes, some tiny, others 30 m (100') long. Many dinosaurs, such as the Stegosaurs, Triceratops, Brontosaurs and Hadrosaurs, were plant-eaters, while others, such as the Tyrannosaurs, were meat-eaters. The dinosaurs died out 65 million years ago. Many scientists believe this was due to a climate change the dinosaurs could not adjust to.

Yy

Yellowjacket Wasp *with a Garden Spider, Barn Swallows*

Colonies of Yellowjackets, a common type of wasp, are primarily made up of egg-laying queens and female workers. Late in the season a few males arrive to fertilize young queens who, unlike the others, hibernate over winter.

In the spring, the young queens build "starter" nests with "wasp paper" (chewed up wood bits mixed with saliva) which their offspring will complete over the summer. By early fall, the nest may contain several thousand cells and two thousand wasps, all of whom will die when the cold comes except for a few select young queens.

Zz

Zoo *(border repeats animals A-Z)*

1. Ruby-Throated Hummingbird
2. Brown Bat
3. Zebra Butterfly
4. American Redstart
5. Chickadee
6. Grizzly Bear
7. Magpie
8. Walrus
9. Groundhog
10. White-Tailed Deer
11. Mountain Goat
12. Pronghorn Antelope
13. Caribou
14. Muskox
15. Pileated Woodpecker
16. Wolf
17. Bighorn Sheep
18. Bobcat
19. Porcupine
20. Skunk
21. Barn Owl
22. Opossum with young
23. Hare
24. Badger
25. Massasauga Rattler
26. Toad
27. Box Turtle
28. Wood Duck
29. Yellow Perch
30. Brook Trout
31. Painted Turtle
32. Lake Sturgeon
33. Crayfish